Welcome to
Little Funnies

Little Funnies is a delightful collection of picture books made to put a giggle into storytime.

There are funny stories about a laughing lobster, a daring mouse, a teeny tiny woman, and lots more colourful characters!

Perfect for sharing, these rib-tickling tales will have your little ones coming back for more!

TEE HEE!

HA HA!

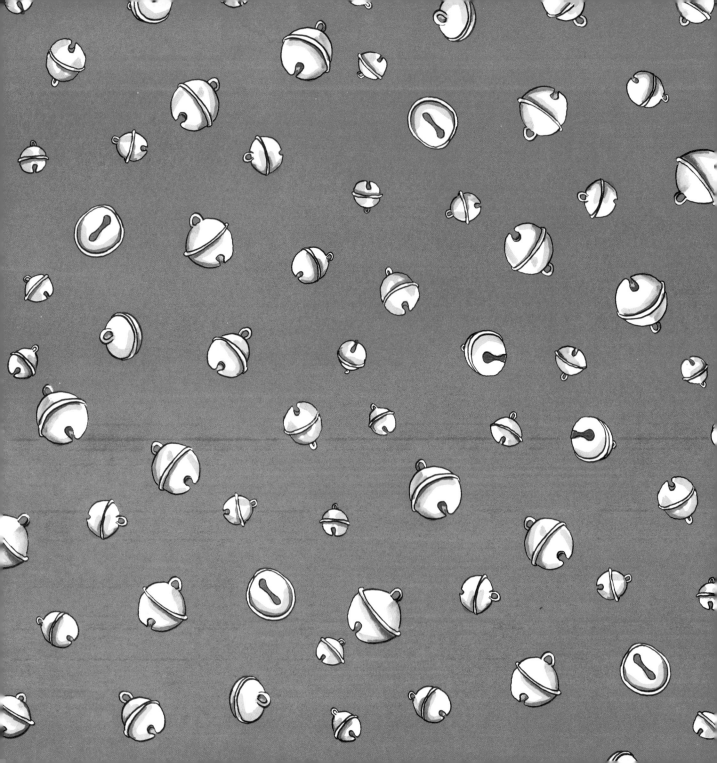

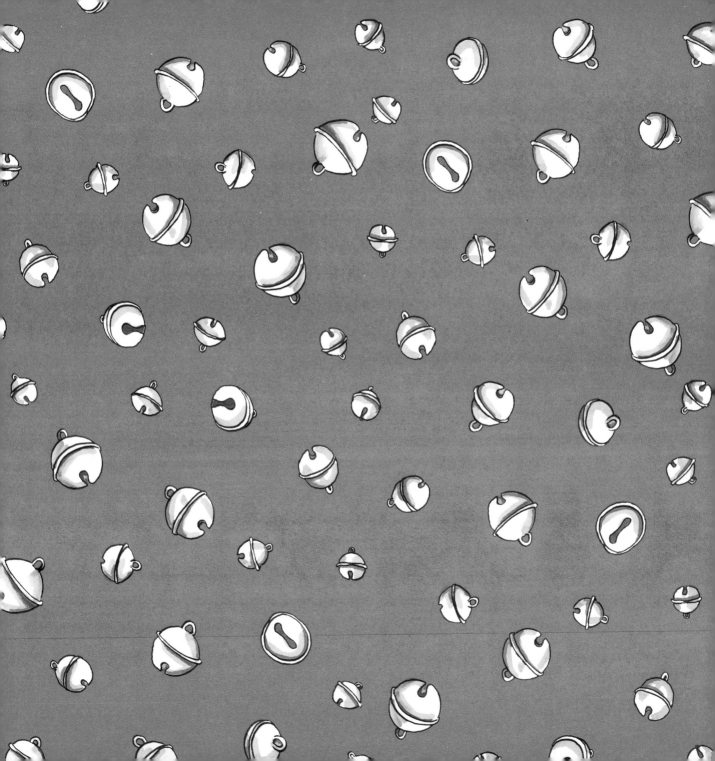

For Fergus

First published 1995 by Walker Books Ltd
87 Vauxhall Walk, London SE11 5HJ

This edition published 2007

10 9 8 7 6 5 4 3 2 1

© 1995 Anita Jeram

The moral rights of the illustrator
have been asserted.

This book has been typeset in Columbus.

Printed in China

British Library Cataloguing in Publication Data:
a catalogue record for this book
is available from the British Library.

ISBN 978-1-4063-0793-1

www.walkerbooks.co.uk

Anita Jeram

Daisy Dare

WALKER BOOKS
AND SUBSIDIARIES

LONDON • BOSTON • SYDNEY • AUCKLAND

Daisy Dare did things
her friends were far too
scared to do.
"Just dare me," she said.
"Anything you like.
I'm never, *ever* scared!"

So they dared her to walk
the garden wall.

They dared her to eat a worm.

They dared her to stick out her tongue at Miss Crumb. And she did!

One day,
Daisy's friends
thought of a really
scary dare to do.

They whispered it to Daisy.
"I'm not doing that!" she said.
"Daisy Dare-not!" they laughed.

Daisy took a deep breath. "All right," she said. "I'll do it." This was the dare: to take the bell off the cat's collar.

The cat was asleep. That was good.

The bell slipped off easily. That was good too.

But Daisy's hands trembled so much that the bell tinkled, the cat woke up ...

and that was
very,
very
bad!

Daisy ran and ran
as fast as she could,
back to her friends,
through the
garden

gate, and into the house
where the cat
couldn't follow.

"Phew!" said Billy.
"Wow!" gasped Joe.
"You're the bravest,
most daring mouse in the whole
world!" shouted Contrary Mary.
Daisy Dare grinned with pride.
"Just dare me," she said.
"Anything you like…

I'm only *sometimes* scared!"

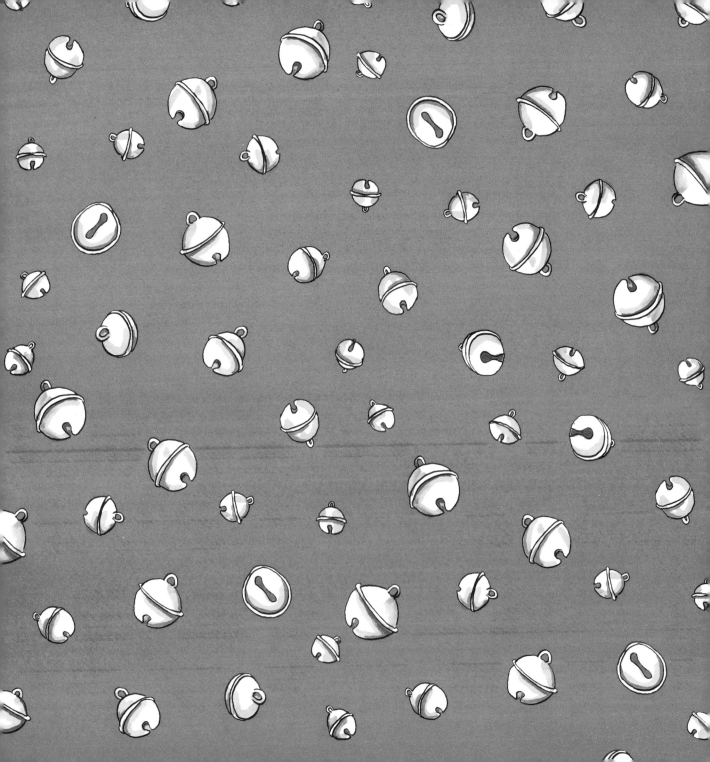

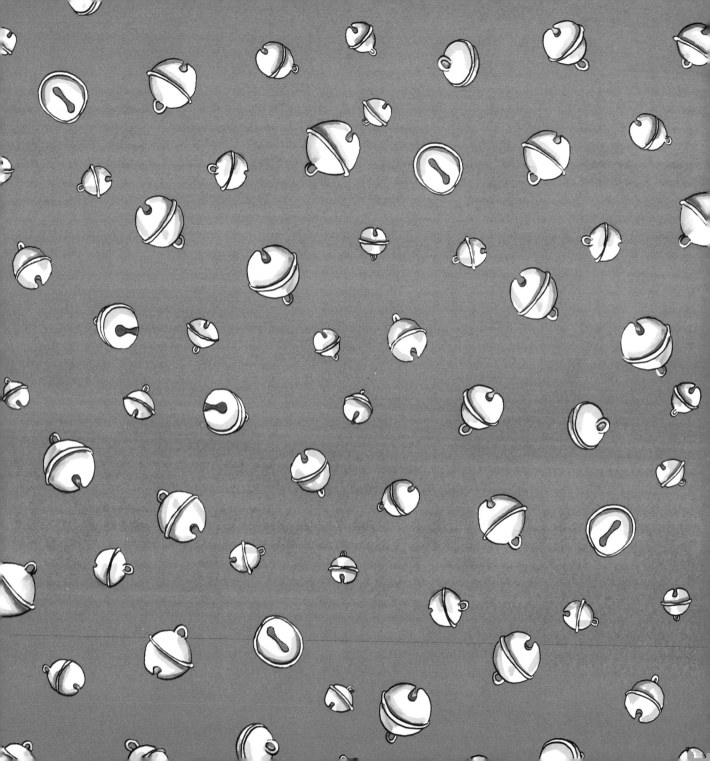